Willy the Champ

Anthony Browne

WALKER BOOKS
AND SUBSIDIARIES
LONDON • BOSTON • SYDNEY • AUCKLAND

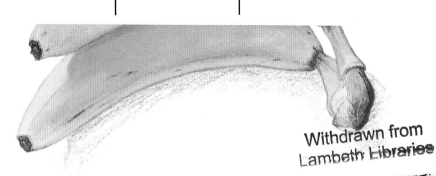

For Ellen

First published 1985 by Julia MacRae Books

This edition published 2008 by Walker Books Ltd
87 Vauxhall Walk, London SE11 5HJ

12 14 16 18 17 15 13 11

© 1985 Anthony Browne

The right of Anthony Browne to be identified as author-illustrator of this work has been
asserted by him in accordance with the Copyright, Designs and Patents Act 1988

This book has been typeset in Plantin

Printed in China

British Library Cataloguing in Publication Data:
a catalogue record for this book is available from the British Library

ISBN 978-1-4063-1873-9

www.walker.co.uk

Willy didn't seem to be any good at anything.

He liked to read . . .

and listen to music . . .

and walk in the park with his friend, Millie.

Willy wasn't any good at soccer . . .

He did try.

Willy tried bike racing . . .

He really did try.

Sometimes Willy walked to the pool.

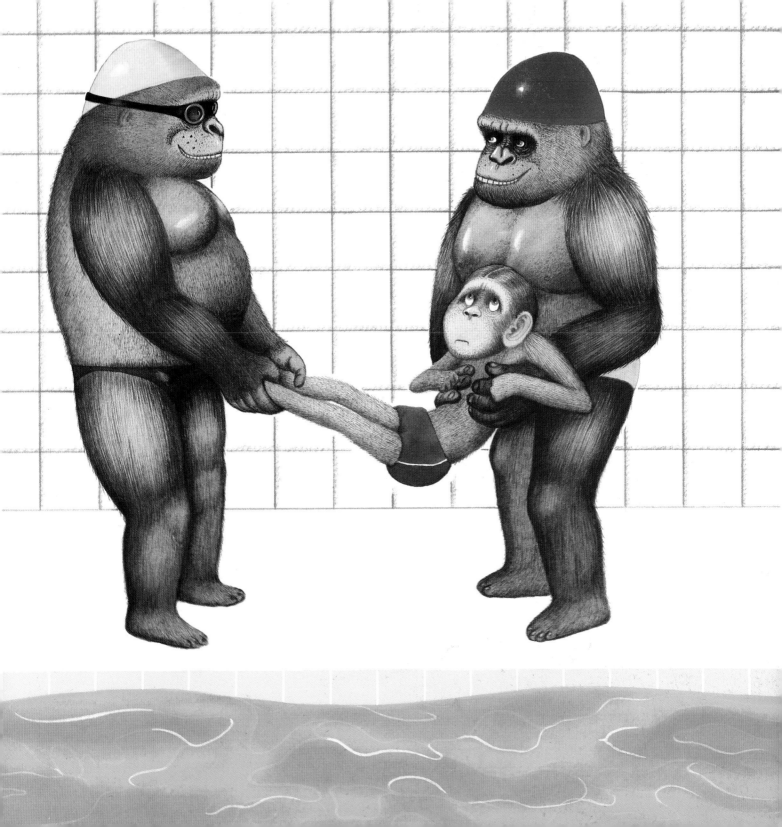

Other times he went to the cinema with Millie.

But it was always the same. Nearly everyone
laughed at him – no matter what he did.

One day Willy was standing on the corner with the boys when a horrible figure appeared.

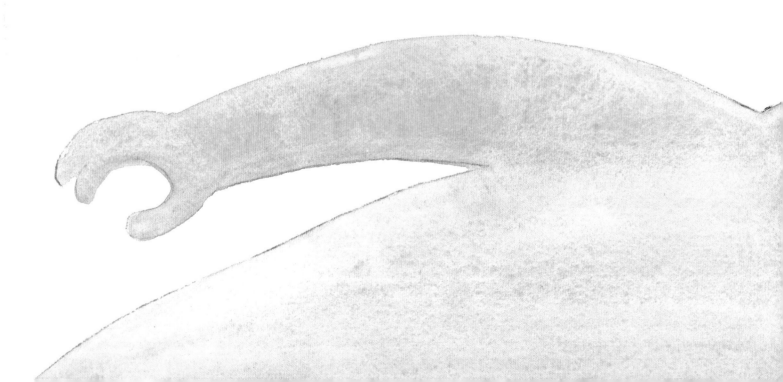

It was Buster Nose.
And he *had* a horrible figure.
The boys fled.

Buster threw a vicious punch.

Willy ducked . . .

. . . then he stood up!

"Oh, I'm sorry," said Willy, "are you alright?"

Buster went home to his mum.

Willy was the Champ.